You Are the Phenomenology

D1520629

# You Are the Phenomenology

TIMOTHY O'KEEFE

University of Massachusetts Press
AMHERST AND BOSTON

ISBN 978-1-62534-351-2 (paper)

Set in Iowan Old Style BT Pro
Printed and bound by Maple Press, Inc.

Cover design by Patricia Duque Campos
Cover photo *Wash Day,* by Walker Evans.
The Metropolitan Museum of Art, Gift of Arnold H. Crane, 1972 (1972.742.12)
© Walker Evans Archive, The Metropolitan Museum of Art

Library of Congress Cataloging-in-Publication Data

Names: O'Keefe, Timothy, 1979– author.
Title: You are the phenomenology / Timothy O'Keefe.
Description: Amherst : University of Massachusetts Press, 2018. | Series:
Winner of the Juniper Prize for Poetry |
Identifiers: LCCN 2017050259 (print) | LCCN 2017059724 (ebook) | ISBN
9781613765920 (e-book) | ISBN 9781613765937 (e-book) | ISBN 9781625343512
(pbk.)
Subjects: LCSH: Experimental poetry, American. | Experimental literature,
American.
Classification: LCC PS3615.K46 (ebook) | LCC PS3615.K46 A6 2018 (print) | DDC
811/.6—dc23
LC record available at https://lccn.loc.gov/2017050259


British Library Cataloguing-in-Publication Data
A catalog record for this book is available from the British Library.

*to Xhenet*
*for all the reasons I know you know*
*and all the ones I don't*

# CONTENTS

# ACKNOWLEDGMENTS

Many thanks to Dara Wier, James Haug, Mary Dougherty, Sally Nichols, Dawn Potter, and everyone at the University of Massachusetts Press for their vision and support. Grateful acknowledgment is made to the editors of the following journals in which many of these texts (or variations thereof) first appeared: *American Poetry Review, Colorado Review, FIELD, Gulf Coast, MARY, Massachusetts Review, New American Writing, Offending Adam, Paris-American Review, Salt Hill, Seneca Review,* and *VOLT.*

Like everyone, I've been helped along the way. The varieties and magnitudes are impossible to track. In the conception and encouragement of this book, a few stand out: Geoffrey Babbitt, Elizabeth Byron, Kate Coles, Kathryn Cowles, Craig Dworkin, Davy Gibbs, Brian Hitselberger, Jason Lemire, Rebecca Lindenberg, Susan McCarty, Jacob Paul, D. A. Powell, Paisley Rekdal, Donald Revell, and Thomas Wilcox. You are heroes, all.

Finally, to my parents: the pages begin with you.

You Are the Phenomenology

# SHAPE INTO SONG

Your face before me is an
epiphany for distance and crossing.

—*Mei-mei Berssenbrugge*

## PINWHEEL

Poem with a patter, a pat of butter, the utter shake & scrawl of
it, fitter than snow, sown or soaking, a king with a Play-Doh
crown, a crow in the tulips, the lips you've touched, as ouch is
all, all in an earring, a ring for the rosy, the roseate leaves, &
leave the door when you go. Gone with a kettle glow, a lowing,
a wing in the thunder, *asunder asunder* say the stars, the tar in
the road. Odes to unbecoming, come to me, tome of lost letters,
steer : flee, leeward fly the linnets, the lint traps, the tropes for
sky, Kyrie, Valkyrie, Erie is burning, the urns brimming over.
Verdant shoes, hoe the garden, ardent angel, angle of forgetful-
ness, forge a knot, not undone please not. Note: the Ottoman
Empire fell on a languid evening, evensong, Eve twined in
flowers, a lowering flag, a lagging summer, a sum of spectacled
things, hinge wisteria, the wistful bottle (ocean's middle), a
mile-long valentine, tines of a missing fork, for no one, none,
non. On a Sunday, sun for the portico, port for the clipper.
Clap-off emotion, tie me a moon, moo me a cow, a coward
season, a son of a son of a son, a songstress, a tress tied to the
grate, a rat in the wall, & all are come under weather, under-
water. Wear the raspberry sweater. Sweet is the sunburnt offal,
if offhanded, if hand-me-down, if down go the paper boats,
the oatmeal breakfasts, the feasts, the fasts. At last our hearing bespeaks the heard: the hardening, the den of winter, a tin
heart, thin tear in the shining sleeve. *Leave the door* I said. Said
*When you go.*

# SONG FOR YOU WHO TURN THE PAGE

You are not a Quaker farmer
and I have no prophetic ankle
we can trust.

But the way your reading
finger rides the page
is not unlike
a harrow
and this makes all
my minerals
keen.

It is strange labor—
building dirt in the dark.

We've learned the annular views
squarely. Cropped to the point
of symbol—
this the gyroscope
that the bystander
not waving
at the hot-air balloon
where we now live.

It need not be a child staring out
of a charcoal suit.
It need not portend.
We can see no
one knows
how to die

and we will bear the sound
the world between
we will find that

something

        shudders back
back from out of all
we've never been.

# BURIED SONG

Desire the glass surface of completion.
Desire to break in someone's hands.

Desire this
        hum in the powerlines
        tip-top the maypole
        distance, a traveling color

or lips that pronounce
the length you think for *limousine.*

What we were spoken through
    a felon syllable
        that night & others—
        solitary candle, a drinking jar
        we shared out of shyness
so that our mouths might touch.

        *Now* is a hole in the saying.
Desire the point of broken reference.

Release the snow from its coming round.
    Storm is
        *outcropping*
    the day.

Spine, finger, portal—
        desire plants a bell for the daffodils—
    amazed root, among, among.

# QUADRILATERAL : AMORATIC

Bees bumble, cumulus ensues, and that's the new precision :
They hailed for love, an October grammar, the linking orchard :
The opposite of *agency* is *weathervane* :
Show us again, the ripening. Show us what fell.

## QUADRILATERAL : ADULT LULLABIES

Chitchat and highballs. Thus the decades, plush as zeppelins :

Rivering peal, rivering whorl, shut-eye river we swallow that pearl :

Occasionally, in heaven, their eyes drift downward to the thought
    of heaven :

She lights the mossy walk. Steals the tongue from his every tower.

## QUADRILATERAL : FIRE PROVES THE EFFIGY

Be my Janus, my monolith, my tiny steps along the plank :

As usual, the previous tenant's mice were flourishing :

Chuck an orange and there's your meteor :

It's motion we dream, not pictures. A smoke ring laureling, not a
   crown.

## QUADRILATERAL : DESIRE ON THE ATOLL

I was crudely drawn up at the time. All torso and teeth, translucent :
The peony stems hoist petals they cannot finally heft :
She missed him in graffiti dreams and conch shells. That that was
    all of it :
Glass frontiers, and still we swim with our hands cupped.

# SONG BEYOND CONVICTION

*to Xhenet*

You were a strong epoch
and folkloric surround.
The desert-spanning caravan

     and garlands
     and garlands

none of them final.
Daytime begins the day.

You were humming
a song I once praised

     in words for
     its words and

it was then—
a beach afternoon, sand in our hair—
you would start me forgetting.

# TRANSPARENT SONG

Summer, our becoming
garment that conceals
what it perfectly shows.

The downhill bay bristling,
a bead of sweat on the chin.
We've traveled continents

within the brake and brackish
noise our bodies make
and we've slept the way out.

People with smaller people,
the harbor all a-teeter.
The night before, someone

mentioned Lowell at the sight
of skunks tunneling under a fence.
Each its own rite, thoroughgoing,

and a drive down the coast is wind
inevitable, the heard-from times
greet us in a gravel parking lot.

That there were pelicans, mangy
shrubberies, a bridge—it was stray talk
straining for an end.

We made our best
rain-a-day faces, we
who had weathered perfection.

Had anyone noticed blankets
dangling from the trees?
Glass blankets.

It wasn't us, but we were looking,
and that's the vision we'd keep—
simple, strenuous.

## LOOM SONG

Counted 37 steps to

        the mulberry tree.

    Fewer and fewer—you

        grew into you, your

        treadle and reed, warped

in the fragrant weave berries float. You

    now harness substantial air,

        the common crush of seasons.

    When the steps swell again

shuttling low into further

    summer summer summer

ends. You are not the first.

# SONG FOR YOU WHO ARE STILL AFRAID

Your death, its hum and flail, we love your death.
Death of pleasure, death of censure, death
of the blink and blank stare. Death that whimpers,
death that kneels, death that vamps in the produce aisle,
death with a storm's eye for the tremulous field.
Falling death blizzard death electric death—they are yours,
all, swift as the river flushes minnows from your hair.
Death with vermin, death with benefits, death in the quiver
and the creel (death keeps reeling reeling the abyssal hook),
death with a keepsake odor, death in the subway shine
of a consultant's loafers. Plain death out of plain air, death
that measures the string death severs, death if by land and death if by sea
and death if by silence of the coal-mine canary. Death as the shineboy
who takes up the singing.
                                  Your death preens, your death barters,
your death flatters the very paint from the walls.
Your death mimics other deaths, other lives full of that same
autumn fullness that would never end, as your death never ends,
as your death ends. Kingly death, carnival death, death without
a harpist to lull death from here though none hail from here.
Death that mourns you, death that preserves you, death that dies
waiting for what night will create you. (Death does admire its
    forfeitures.)
Silicone death, Lycra death, death at the time-share pavilion,
at the resort casino, its compound eye glaring, glaring
not at you but death all the same, all the same you die
pedicured in a Kevlar vest, rabid in a spread collar, scattered
in the city's lone aspen grove, a scene on Achilles' shield,
and so your death floods the fields of Troy—they are waiting there
still, the stately ships dotting your horizon, like toys, like tinsel,
none swelling windward, none plaintive in the whirlpool,
none fastening you to the mast, ears waxed over, and so your death
fares well, fares terribly well.
                                  Your death suits you, it tangoes close,
it's no kiss-and-tell. We love your death and we love its love

for you, the way your death hones itself beneath
the death you know, the death-not-you, the death you
stock and serve, the death you martyr, the death you will
always deserve. Please know that your death
is quick to learn discretion, your death is true
to its first word, your death is an island, a shell, a souvenir
on the porch of a Nebraskan family, a moon fogged over
by the breath of their spoiled poodle. Please don't ever, ever
worry. Your death won't neglect you, though your death
does forget its chores, its grooming, how many rooms
it's built for you and how many doors, each a slightly different
hue, an infinite green, and how can you possibly solve
the maze of your death? Or do you imagine some sliver
and shade your death has not conceived, wet paint on the door
of a hidden room, a plush sofa, a poem you believe
you can live through?

## QUADRILATERAL : NEBULA

Love was an asteroid covered in asters. We were close enough to see :
One makes promises to combat omens. One does not make omens :
Impersonal yet intimate, as in *That's the hollowest shirt I've ever seen* :
You die one day. Once. Someone's future memory, origins out of view.

## QUADRILATERAL : BECKONING EPITAPH

All wash and welter and the creek can't quiet its dulcimer :

Mid-distance, a figure turns, stays turning :

The least of night fills this broken bowl :

The capital galleries dim together. One portrait keeps winking.

## QUADRILATERAL : RED-HANDED BLUE

Lend me your brutes, your Dargers, your unlessonable pains :

We chose the hotel but not the selves that entered :

I love you the way a severed head loves a serving tray :

Dogs play and play their game into being. God is simpler than that.

## QUADRILATERAL : AND ORPHEUS WAS NEVER SO OLD

Crows will be crows. They skim and scatter you, who knows :
Soft hands, soft thought. The farthest earlobe you ever touched :
Outside, the mob gathers its silence like a bell :
Kicking cans in the mustard light. Back and gone. Going back.

# SONG BEGINNING WITH A LINE BY AGEE

*Now is the night one blue dew.*
Now the festival strewn in swelter—
air teasing air from crickets,
from forgiveness, the gape-mouthed
hangar swimming fireflies and sounds
so familiar you can never really know.

Tomorrow must go must always go
and so we are kept away. The wind passes
through its presence, sewing its tatters
to you, and there are people long
since dozing, people just starting to.

*Of aestival body,* let us now praise
the low-circling comet, the apostates, the mind
that floats its lanterns house to house. I too
was freighted. I too skirted each
call to shelter, was marooned
by the work of portraiture—far figures
grown large, the stooped light
and approach, where a man with denim eyes
stops to tie his shoe, props his heel
on a hydrant—the color you choose.

What was here was before.
Twilight and fog and flowers darkening
in their beds. I never knew the names,
the pedigreed origins, the logic
of soil and seasonality, all due
in their coming round, though today's
dead will be dead tomorrow,
almost the same. Will be tomorrow.
But the flowers, the rickety flowers,
refuse to be any other thing.

# BELLWETHER SONG

Snow the smothering element.

A birdbath, a thousand, all in heaping measure the same.

People coax their winter layers, oil on the skin, and such a regal
    pace—the seasons we wore, the countrysides, twig-wise the
    living, fat sprig of that sobering.

Water in motion is often white.

Others and later will ask *How do we go from*—and July expands
    with the shapely brilliance of a hard hat sunk to the
    bottom of a pond, for example.

Or, in the motile shade of palms and pinions they create, we nap
    with shells in our bathing suits.

This is a way of getting below without delving, time-as-usual, the
    open aperture.

Now you're walking through and much older.

The moon is a literal nightlight, a revealer, though you'll go on
    imagining hallways.

The mountains are the first to know—in this, you can't turn back.

Water in motion is often white.

Daybreak hoards color from snow, but only color.

You can exert yourself there, you can flee, you can fall back to
    sleep in the foyer.

The thaw takes everything in its release.

With nothing left to hold, the birdbaths rush skyward.

Falling and falling is an exact being.

# SONG FOR THE LAST MASSACRE

You remember.
It was late fall.
Maybe winter.
There was talk
of talk at supper
so we froze our words
honed them smooth
as a lake and skated
whole weeks over.

But the images draw
a circle that still
circles
like tadpoles
and they're caught
waiting
for the thaw
the landfall
a night the nets
are hauled finally in
all grit and glimmer

a night without god
to serve the erasure.

# SONG WITH A FOUND TROMBONE

You find the lore
to live in what
will never be yours.

This cat's-eye on the sill,
a first lemon ribbon.
It lights us back
to kindle
the rechildrening.

Cars go to the mountain, mountains
wait for their lifting. Like
a wind. The very noise you see.

Now the princedom now the age.
Strewn gaze to glass go down.
Gutbucket, marigold,
down down—

it calls and calls.
This last ladder, intact.
Pond up from its brass burrow.

# QUADRILATERAL : ALMOST SKIPPING

Mind in its rucksacks, low-slung :

The survivors woke in a woolen green sweater :

Let's be out-of-doors today, let's jaunt :

Sing-song or stowaway—one moth blizzards the night.

# QUADRILATERAL : GREEN NIGHT

Something itches the years-ago, wallpapered rooms, an exacting
  pattern :

People pass by people passing for themselves passing people :

That the dead we convey within might carry us on without :

Dawn. Building. Sheer. Height. I was just myself today.

# YOU ARE THE PHENOMENOLOGY

As a result, fields of experiences are observable and distinguishable and, in the light of the great variety of its relations, one self-identical experience can play a role in several fields at the same time. It is thus that in a certain context of associates one experience would be classed as a physical phenomenon, while in another setting it would figure as a fact of consciousness, almost as one self-identical particle of ink can belong simultaneously to two lines—one vertical and the other horizontal—provided the particle is situated at their intersection.

—*William James*

Imagine that you're an insatiable reader—poetry, fiction, philosophy, plays, history, noir, CNF, DIY, cookbooks, travelogues, comic books, blogs, clickbait scrolling ad infinitum. Reading for you is no mere habit and, on some level, not even a proper activity, but a kind of experiential osmosis that positions language as primary and generative in the world to which it refers. You've always been struck by the elegance of that paradox, its call for exploration. One byproduct of reading this way is that you've acquired a prodigious vocabulary. That's natural enough (and can't be helped), but another consequence that appeared somewhere in the osmotic flux is your desire to focus and channel it all toward some aesthetic end. Therein lies the first gauntlet.

Beyond that, it gets worse. Over the many years of your less abstracted moods, you've become aware of the alchemical effect that language can have on otherwise normal social situations. And this makes you think back on the times you've laughed too loudly, flirted too earnestly, or consigned yourself to brazen silences, the family all around and shooting looks over the holiday roast as you stare into your little well of gravy. However, after a stint of writing and reflection, you do find that you'd like to share your outlook with a friend, someone who's both similar and dissimilar to you, and this makes sense, feels right, since you've always envisioned the whole literary enterprise to be, at bottom, a collaborative enterprise, one that fosters a palpable boon in our understanding of what it means to be human. This, but also a vast, interpretive mire with countless systems of semantic ambiguity whose very purpose seem to be, at times, the enforcement of some totalizing Ambiguity that brooks no definitive claims, no true resting places. So—this, in light of that—there you are, now, ready to listen and be listened to. It's an afternoon in mid-October. Brisk with a bit of tooth. You entered the cafe through a side door and quickly surveyed the room. You found your way to the back, made your salutations, shed your coat, and settled into the corner booth. Your interlocutor begins.

She is a classically trained singer and she speaks with a singer's reserve, one that knows and fears the strain of full-throatedness. She wears a green scarf patterned with gilt parrots. It is easy and safe to look at, but you can't just stare at her collarbone and expect to set a tone of candor and sensitivity. You must look up, at her. You must make eye contact—essential and intricate, concrete and wildly suggestive, the most exacting of all listening skills. Furthermore, your eye contact must be deployed in discrete intervals, and these intervals need to be tailored to your specific interlocutor, the gravity of the subjects under discussion, the nature of your relationship with said interlocutor, the circumstances of the meeting, the time of day, the temperature, the barometric pressure, the kind of week she seems to be having, the kind of week you seem to be having, and please be apprised that all of these variables are chain-linked and coordinated, which means none of them can be calculated before the conversation takes the shape of its unique moment, which means you're going to have to be optically nimble and vigilant and precise if you want what you've always thought of as your *listening practice* to shine through in a way that makes your interlocutor feel completely at ease and unsuspecting of the terrible demands that listening places on you and, frankly, anyone who's mindful of it. So, try to act natural. Sit straight but don't be stiff. Nod your head but not continuously—you're not a guidance counselor. Don't cross your arms against your chest—that expresses doubt, mistrust—and don't rest your folded hands against your belly—that's smug and creepy and paternal. Best to keep your hands on the table. Palms down, of course. If you've got grit under your fingernails, make soft fists. If not, you can let your fingers stretch out a bit, but loosely and with a curve at the knuckle. Keep them still but not statuesque, and don't fuss with the sugar packets.

Now your interlocutor has finished talking. Her face is slightly flushed, her eyes bluer than before, and her elbows are on the table with one hand supporting her chin. You have been good, you can see it for yourself—she turns to you in a pose of quiet relief and gives a half-smile. Her green scarf nearly glows. It is your turn to speak. Imagine, now, that your interlocutor is an exquisite listener, the one from whom you absorbed, without even trying (at least at first), all the best attributes of your listening practice, and the one from whom, you must admit, you still have much to learn. The silent ball is in her court, and so you must begin. Of course you can't just say any rote thing that comes to mind in order to observe her listening prowess and further hone your own practice. You have to reciprocate, you want to reciprocate, and in order to do that, you have to give yourself fully to the speaking act, the one that will convince your interlocutor of the comfort and vulnerability that she has engendered in you, the one that will engender in her those intangible listening responses that you have yet to learn. But, again, make it natural or else it won't work. Not only will it (the conversation) not work, but its breakdown will introduce a rupture in the otherwise seamless, symbiotic rapport that you've both enjoyed, on and off, for years. Now, in the intervening moments that feel impossibly dilated, you find that you don't have an appropriate response to or segue from your interlocutor's speech act, which was compelling and honest and emotionally rich—so much so that it now seems to retreat into its own hermetic bastion, a kind of set piece that wants nothing more than to be acknowledged from a respectful distance. And this is no surprise—after all, your interlocutor is also a superlative orator, one who can modulate between public and private discourses and, more importantly, one who understands that in order to do the work of good listening, one must have something of significant scope and clarity to latch onto, that one simply cannot exercise the entire complex of gestures, looks, and body language on the topic of celebrity divorces or unseasonable weather. So you begin. It's a tentative maundering at first, but your interlocutor is patient. She is aware of her own towering presence and the difficulty of each sea-level beginning. Slowly the scale is laid, the blueprint is drawn, and your words start to amass and career and conjoin within their centrifugal focus. You are watching her watch you. She blinks almost when you blink. She chuckles spontaneously. You both nod for a refill of coffee, and in this, even your silences agree. The sentences come easily now, fluidly, and you start to experience a kind of insular hearing whereby your words pass through a filter that is so deft and responsive that it doesn't feel like a filter at all. It feels like some ideal replica of you, thinking and talking outside of itself but also from deeply within. You can hear what you say before you say it. You can hear your own voice translating itself into itself. It is going well, isn't it. Yes, it is, she says in a look that holds you for an extra second, not quite erotic though it's hard to imagine a half-measure, and that's what makes it perfect. Yes, it is going well.

But now, just when you've settled into the warmth of her reception, you begin to hear a glitch in the dark machinery of your own speech, and this glitch appears in its outermost mechanism—the fact that you yourself are also an external listener of the things you say. What you've been saying amounts to a diatribe against familial duty, which, once you've heard its outward form, you realize is just a conceptually souped-up lament against your older brother for snapping on you last July and later refusing to apologize. Granted, the causal chain leading up to that event is rife with subtext and interpretive blind spots that are themselves delicate and involuted, but let's face it: it's all tediously familiar to pretty much anyone who has active sibling relationships into adulthood. Somewhere along the way, your post-filter-not-yet-external voice has shifted gears or direction or you're not sure what, but it's no longer refining and pacing your own speech act; no, it now seems to imbue the words with a mild sneer, an ironic twang, barely noticeable at first, but you can feel it accelerating and you start to panic at the thought that your internal filter, which just a minute ago seemed a humble and apt servant, has somehow remapped its own circuitry and now threatens to undermine not just your interlocutor's nascent belief that *things are indeed going very well* (as her right hand tucked a lock of hair behind her ear and she dragged her fingertips lightly along her neck, so lightly that you could feel your pinkie ghosting its response along the lip of the creamer), but also your own long-standing conviction that language is the great arbiter of the world and, by harnessing it, we can perform our histories, actuate our futures, and finally concede that so much of the rest is not ours to navigate. Language as the one and the many, the first and the last, the very presence we live through—here but also distantly, like the mirage of water on a summer highway. Is its vanishing the same for everyone, you've often wondered, or is each person subject to a singular distance? No doubt you've met many people and some of them also work their language like a chisel struck by the mallet of their will, but you also get the feeling that some people (maybe even a lot of people) use their presence to assert not just the unimpeachable sharpness of their chisel's edge, but the apparent rectitude of their character for having merely uttered the words. This is to say: a lot of people stake their language to a site of moral power and then coyly invite you to stop by and make yourself at home as if their insignia weren't emblazoned on every wall and threshold.

You know you've met these people, and you know others have met them too. Maybe with even greater aversion. (Over the years, you've come to believe that education is, in its broadest sense, the granting of permission to speak your will and to offer presence, without the fear of being rendered invisible. Not a corpus of knowledge, not a skill set, and certainly not a license to grandstand or pontificate, but a steady belief in the legitimacy of one's identity. You've come to realize that this is *your* site of power—the one you've coveted and valorized, the one whose precincts have, in return, sheltered and galvanized you, and even now, as the internal voice transmutes into an externalizing self, you can feel another stake thrust into the ground, no matter if the ground now feels as though it's turning to sand. This is the sinking feeling you feel—the awareness that some presences may inevitably negate others, that negation is surely the worst aggression one can inflict on another, that every chisel defaces before it creates.

Nonetheless, you can't deny that you are proud of your pedigreed education, not for the velvet on your doctoral robes or the perks of your alumni credit card, but because it took quite a bit of rerouting and recalibration for any of that to appear among your possible horizons, and the fact that you accomplished this first, formative task says more about you than any transcript ever will. This is a thought you like to think, and in a few cavalier moments, you've actually spoken it aloud. You're not proud of those moments, though you can't say you wholly regret them either.) You can now feel your face taking color, you feel the opposite of invisible, and so you pause, catch the server's attention, and order an iced tea. Moments later, it arrives having already sweated through the glass.

And so, no, not *maybe*—the more you think about it—but *probably*: those who wield language from a site of moral power are very probably met by others with greater aversion than you yourself have shown. Or, now, as you think harder and closer and come to the real crux of things, you-can-absolutely-bet-your-ass-on-it with much greater aversion. And so the likelihood that you are less repulsed by these people than others are—does this make you one of them, regardless of the site to which you pledge your allegiance? No, you think, that's a bit presumptuous, self-flagellating, there are some logical steps missing there, etc., but might it not mean that you are inclined toward using language in this way, as a kind of lexical producer? Or is this unpleasant solidarity yet more evidence for your savvy as a lexical consumer—that your empathy is capacious enough to include those whom you consider dangerous and manipulative bloviators of public opinion? Maybe. But, then again, to even begin to think *your empathy is capacious enough*— doesn't that smack of a narcissistic posturing that would preclude any sincere attempt to absorb the world from someone else's less grandiloquent station? Perhaps the obvious conclusion is to cut out the prolix bullshit and just talk about stuff in a way that (A) others can readily apprehend and (B) doesn't make you sound like the aloof, self-satisfied intellectual that you are dead-set against.

To state the big questions in simplest terms—isn't that the goal? And yet a deep-seated part of you—the same part that urged you toward a liberal-arts education and an ecumenical world-view and a masochistic work ethic and the embrace of all things strange and mundane—this part senses that many issues have no denominator that is truly common to all parties involved. This part of you knows that the aforementioned Ambiguity of words and the structures they create is often irreducible, and while we may agree that this is axiomatic, the way of the world, not much doing there, etc., we still have the Herculean task of reconciling the innumerable lenses through which people perceive the world around them and inject their presence within it. And so, after much attentive listening, if your interlocutor now says that a rectangle defines some situation that you've always considered octagonal (so to speak), what's the use of debating how it fits into the larger mosaic whole? Can we even assume that such a whole exists when the foundation often appears not just in rubble, but in multiform rubble? If the whole is merely the sum of contiguous experience, if each of us is confined to some half-swept corner of isolated consciousness—*where the dogs go on with their doggy life,* where the chance that any two thought-vectors meet head-on is roughly equivalent to the odds that two randomly chosen cars will arrive at the same remote crossroads at exactly the same day and hour and instance of their lifetime trajectories—then what was the point of all that unquenchable reading?

You've now spoken at length, and it is very hard to map an emotional hierarchy in the things you've said, never mind trace the desultory path between those things. And yet you can't shake the feeling that your internal filter has done right, that this is how things *are,* that your inability to encapsulate even the minor trials of everyday life says something crucial about the experience of language and what it really means to be present with others. Not to mention what it says about your so-called site of power. Your server brings the bill on a metal dish. He has drawn a smiley face at the bottom and discreetly covered the total with two peppermints. You now feel clear and cleared, and you begin to wonder if there is such a thing as transparency that is pure enough to render one invisible and hypervisible at the same time, a polestar that offers opposite roads out of the wilderness—both begin on mossy escarpments that descend into forest, both wend through shade flowers and waving boughs, both are mottled in the light and dark patches they've passed through when they open, at last, as all things must open, on the same native valley. You look up, as if through trees, and find that your interlocutor is staring right at you, unblinking. You have never seen her in this face. It is taut at the edges, tinged with gray, and there's a vague contortion to it, not discernible in any one feature but there all the same—a synthetic quality that soaks through her expression as if she were wearing a mask, or as if she were a palimpsest, or as if she had lived and died long ago and been undertaken and very carefully arranged. The mark of your valley is wiped clean off the map. Here, your hands regain their clamminess. Your undershirt sticks to your back. Some realities never leave the body. They are distorted, subsumed, and they are yours alone. How to speak to them, as they are. How to bridge them, when they themselves are the bridging. She does not say, and you cannot think how she would. The parrots on her scarf have alighted and will not turn away.

Your interlocutor stands up and excuses herself to the restroom, palms pressing the sides of her skirt. You watch her weave through the tightly arranged tables, and for the first time, you notice that the cafe is loud and bustling and indifferent. She knocks on the restroom door, disappears inside, and you are now alone in a throng of silverware and water glasses. You wonder why it is so, why it must be so. Then you wonder why the thought had never occurred, until now, that although you have seen wild animals along the highway, in a drought summer, making their cautious approach, bemused at the streaks of fatal cars that race toward latter distances, distance being itself the promise of more—perhaps you were wrong when you thought they had come to cross over. Perhaps this is the mirage they had sought. You can see them there in great masses, crowding the hot asphalt, predator and prey alike, stoic and noble. And perhaps, as if cued by some invisible conductor, something miraculous will happen: the animals will bow their heads together, and they will drink.

# SING INTO SHAPE

On the bridge over the moat, where we lingered for a while, Thomas
Abrams told me how much he liked the ducks, a couple of which were
quietly paddling around in the water and snapping up the food which
he now and then took out of the pocket of his overalls and threw
down for them. I have always kept ducks, he said, even as a child, and
the colours of their plumage, in particular the dark green and snow
white, seemed to me the only possible answer to the questions that are
on my mind. That is how it has been for as long as I can remember.

—*W. G. Sebald*

# QUADRILATERAL : EVERYDAY MARGINALIA

My friend always calls with a crinkled voice that's her now :
I never could imagine a new face. Never deflect what I saw :
The places she'd been, faint canticles, were filters. Were shutters :
Each holds forth, but in abeyance. Interleaves of a misremembered
    book.

## QUADRILATERAL : DOOR AJAR ON THE TOP FLOOR

If we are swaying, then there must be an anchor. Are we swaying :
I lose focus and the world projects. Here is a pitcher without any
    milk :
If there are only thresholds. Be lighthouse, be locomotive :
Last glance at inchoate skies. Here is the shore awash with blue
    paper.

# SONG OF THE SEAGULL EMPIRICIST

1
Welling into night
     its navy swath slow
     to pull the morning updrop
and the summer party falls
to metaphysics.

     The people want balloons
     but not in moonlight
and the people want
moonlight. I am

for the people.
The shadows fulfill us
     and so we are never full.

     Look around. It's a long time
out of the cave.

2
The damn gulls—
look how they alight on open water,
ignoring their roles in divination.

3
That June we carved our names in Newport,
and the tide wound us round the island
to a deserted yacht. Years later they were still there
but not the yacht, years of shard-shells
lapped ashore, our eyes fired green,
seaglassed. Like that, we forget knowing
how to feel, and the sea moves just like a sea,
and when the amassing ship makes
its final turn to windward, the winch

that turns there—as if we lived that breach
in the offing, that whence, nothing like a gull—
turns absently.

**4**
Don't get
any mister ideas says
a sometime dyslexic sister.
It's bad enough that
we and the gulls can both
*pass over a bridge*
and our words will never
confuse our motions.

**5**
Naturalized mortem          today

was woolen to touch

Never found a flock of baby gulls

that first book turning

the child in place      world firm-up


We painted the sunniest wall

and it draped the land

Like wrapping countless scarves          fore

and aft          we eyed our observations

and gifted the birds their eggshell          tremor

and sleep

6

To externalize
one's thought,
     as buildings
     compose the morning,
building
    joist, cornice, arcade.

A farmer burns his autumn field.
          The fire line is a past
          continued and a future
          that continuously arrives.
      The present takes from each

and the farmer watches, his body
startled with rest.
          What is taken away
          is each, and is still
    taken.

## SLUMBERING SONG

Eyelids strobe

        deepwater violets        nearing here and

   are.       Wall, wall.


Light borrows

the world        some tiniest door in the cloister

   and we rush through morning to get

shortened       in breath, a nightly imprint

     beneath the coverlet.

Daytime begins

   the day begins

apart.

Your youth is modular and boring

   into its selves.

Two figures on a hill, walking backlit       heads bowed

a final turn in the clover

     and it always was that far. It was always

   not long.

# QUADRILATERAL : GLASS ELEVATOR

Pink starts, blank carnations, and a man with a beautiful sneeze :

Swam out the hurricane, the town, the untoward allegiances :

Today is named *Forgiveness as a Deco Frame*. No use pretending :

Some days we sleep outside and clear across the chasm.

## QUADRILATERAL : ENTROPY

Ragtime wounds, my friends, ragtime wounds :

The balloon man hoists a mosaic emotion :

Tell us the one about the sinking island—point to the very spot :

*Summer peaches* we said, as if there were another kind.

## QUADRILATERAL : SOLUBLE

Where recollection fails, the body takes a fuller stride :
Like books you keep for the marginalia. A dead friend's boots :
I can listen to the icicles melt and almost no one says much :
We're each given a palm's width of ocean. All the way down.

# QUADRILATERAL : NEW JERSEY AFTER ALL

Postcards and prop planes. Red letters on the sky :
Thirst to meadow, meadow to not-come-back :
Knowledge is a knower, each window's train :
The sand forgives what it cannot fill. Why wait.

# MERCY SONG

My mother was a fish
and would live on.
My father, the downstream
pockets of river boulder,
however many it took.

Time places. Nothing
outside, no remainders,
so let them alone.
They are yours to leave—
a depleted elegy,
fluid blooms of air
rising through water,
and the eventual breach
as all is breached
in the wider-after.

Your head tilts to its thinking.
Sometimes I call you
a portrait of oblivion
but it's more the inside-out.

The swimming hole abides its cold mirror—

and like that, sometimes,
you're the rock-ribbed setting
of a hook.

# CAREENING SONG

gone the sunball
none to fetch it
whose throw was it
flung it there
my bumblebee
my leeward shelter
what shape shaped its
notional weight
how shored
the fire's entropy
how ghostheart the cities
infolded novas
that won't fall away
won't blinker
the orbital path
hardening to a plate
and every wall calls
to that plate

as you too
are thrown you
who shiver
the lawns
into frosthood you
who install winter
pursuant
to stars
and still all
stilled
by this burst arc
of night see
it's not so
grave as all
that
has a date
a mark

# QUADRILATERAL : TUBA EULOGY

How plumb believable the leaves, clinging to winter trees :

Our voices broke to lower octaves. Our thinking would not transpose :

Life on a sphere—every point or no point, an apex :

The new cadets parade in truck beds, white gloves waving.

## QUADRILATERAL : LANDSCAPISM

Coachman blues. How the carriage frames his every view :
Gardeners condition growth. *But some* they say *are weeds.*
Utterance paraphrases the impulse. There's your exit wound :
In the child emperor's dream, every peasant's head was a snowglobe.

# QUADRILATERAL : MISTLESS

Dusk hones the pitch pines, harbors marigold :
The funeral-goers seemed all welded together :
We met the aporias agreeably, the geese honking falsetto :
Rib-shaped moon, seen topwise. How many make a cage.

# QUADRILATERAL : FAMILY BAVARIAN TREE

Tots on rollers, paddling feet, precipice learns the balance :
They say it builds character but never what type :
Sherbet snow in the alpenglow. And now the clouds preen dynastic :
It's a radial measure of good and evil. How many peripheries extend
    to you.

# SONG FROM THE LATE BARBICANS

My fronts were beyond ambush, my bastions cleanly surrendered.
An afternoon of slow textures—moss patch in the turret, a moth
with spring in its fur, and none to scale the oceaning view.
Is it unblemished or healed? (A shoal, a schooner.) They came
at night: the youngest sang madrigals, the oldest sewed buttons
on an infinite shirt. For breakfast, I dressed like a soldier
and all the glassware complied, right down to the icicles.
My fronts were quietest in summer, cleverest in suede.
*They come at night* it was said. Foregone, where
I'm imagining. *Look there* it was said—at the mead hall, at vespers,
such mild faces at the stake—*that's how the spinnakers glow.*

# SONG WITH ROBERT LAX

I recognize your
sun-spooked island

in the years
of becoming what

I can't say.

*What* I say
to the every-

where you are
composing—

*What*
with you there

*What*
with you there—

our see-
sawing crowned

with remedies
and blank particulars.

## QUADRILATERAL : HOME WHERE WE DO NOT THINK TO THINK

Morning peels everything back and the sun's just a little radish :

Life on a houseboat, riding the line of two weathers :

Instinct and action confuse. Thereto the grace of animals :

One night, the dollhouse door opens. The miniatures petrify.

## QUADRILATERAL : IDEAS ABOUT THE THING

What begins is a percept and we are what the percept begins :
Aghast, the war. No trumpet fits this embouchure :
Come March, we'll wake wild and roam the topiary zoo :
That's one history. A box of trophies in a stranger's basement.

# QUADRILATERAL : A THEORY OF LATE TWENTIETH-CENTURY AMERICA

A geriatric labradoodle wakes on a trampoline, the same :

Kids out making nowhere of themselves :

The new-growth sycamores prove a highway ornament :

Twin recliners in TV light. Hushed inside voluble snow.

# QUADRILATERAL : WHARF LIFE

Toes numb in brackish waters but for no great waning :
The rooms were gabardine, were doily. Each a different monogram :
When the men are afraid they are men. Yesterday is tall :
No sailors sank in that thrall, though we still hear it, that brink.

# BLOOD SONG

Trace me simple—
a figure the children can't
not color in, circle
of an unsteady hand—
if never more than this flame
under the hill, a flowering index,
this black dog chasing an atmosphere.

Crayon-lit trunks
crush to paper, millennia to sheaves we
populate—a simpering June,
a julep, some heirloom fear
we couldn't look up
the picture for, the meaning for.

## HOMECOMING SONG WITH AMPELMÄNNCHEN

Because a home travels too—
yellow vessel greening the dark,
as I fumble for a light switch
and touch turns the night of mind.

The dog cranes her neck
in dawdling affection.
Poplar blossoms clot together—
a would-be balm, thrum
and scree, each and all
adrift in the williwaw—
and there is
                no jaywalking in Berlin,
the mores of passage ignited
by small men in bowlers:
half-praying, half-crucified there
in the opposite of *backlight* what
would that be? The first step

in recovering a scene, your place
in its passing, is to curtain
the brilliance of grief.
No sightline can compass that air
though today is hewn clear and
clearing itself from view and
                you can see this
isn't much of a man,
but the shape of one—
absent, legibly.

Here are the cream walls, the tumblers,
doorways unmoored by the humblest beam.
There are no canyons as quiet

as those in the sea,
and the sea is not quiet.

We wandered the Tiergarten. Drank a pilsner.
It was sunny, I think—slanting antique,
the way a headlight turns the hillside.

Never not there, once seen.
And there were women in caftans selling prophecies.
And there were children sprinting naked for the stream.

## QUADRILATERAL : AND PROTEUS WAS A GROUP OF SMALL CHILDREN

Years in the hollowed-out oak, now a cello soundtrack :

That one breaks his nose and gains a friendship :

That one is now her mother's age in some first memory :

We chased night bugs, their will of sound, though the sound had
    none.

## QUADRILATERAL : LINKBOY

The fears of the octopus are clouded in ink. A parable :
Long measure, a child's home. The measure out from :
They were just words on the gravestones, just words :
If it is empty, it is not a mirror. And if it is never empty.

## QUADRILATERAL : PINCH IN YOUR HEEL

Soars the mackled sound, kites ago :

A Polish boy thinks with accordions, adopts a stammer :

When were we first older than we wanted to be :

That was our city, our chisel, the corbeil from which we ate.

# QUADRILATERAL : RELICTION

Our mother in a cantaloupe dress, breezing the sunset through :
The piano calibrates the player. One day, the gait syncopates :
This wayward agency, gable to gable, and some peaks pass us over :
Not events, but atmospheres. Not trains in the night, but whistling.

# EDENIC

We named you the hereafter, the husk,
flag of an unpeopled country.

We declaimed your embattled heights,
a scarlet halo there for the basking

and you would be a hymn torn
from the hymnal, you singly.

Call us back from names, from naming.
River is no river's aspiration

not even in that first falling
sleep, the great mirror, ease

in the floral bower, and though
you speak driftingly

of nascence, of flames, you heed
not these human beatitudes.

We are what follows our lives, tug
and collar, and the waters we've crossed

are slackened, poised. None go further.
It's no longer raining and the rain hasn't stopped.

We've simply walked to the end of it.

# JUNIPER
JUNIPER PRIZE FOR POETRY

This volume is the forty-second recipient of the
Juniper Prize for Poetry, established in 1975 by the
University of Massachusetts Press in collaboration with
the UMass Amherst MFA program for Poets and Writers.
The prize is named in honor of the poet Robert Francis
(1901–1987), who for many years lived in Fort Juniper,
a tiny home of his own construction, in Amherst.

TIMOTHY O'KEEFE is from Manasquan, New Jersey. His education includes degrees from Middlebury College, Johns Hopkins University, and the University of Utah. His first book, *The Goodbye Town*, won the FIELD Poetry Prize and was published by Oberlin College Press in 2011. His poems and lyric essays have appeared in *American Poetry Review, Best American Poetry, Boston Review, Colorado Review, Conjunctions, Denver Quarterly, Seneca Review, VOLT*, and elsewhere. He teaches writing and literature at Piedmont College, where he directs the creative writing program. He lives in Athens, Georgia.

CPSIA information can be obtained
at www.ICGtesting.com
Printed in the USA
LVHW110521080721
692105LV00009B/908

9 781625 343512